Carrot Holes
and
Frisbee Trees

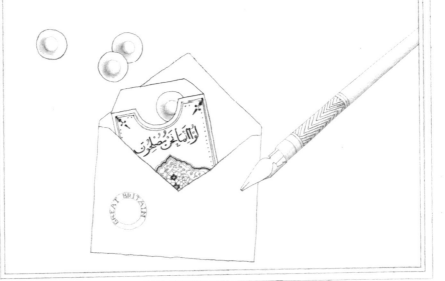

Section of Seed

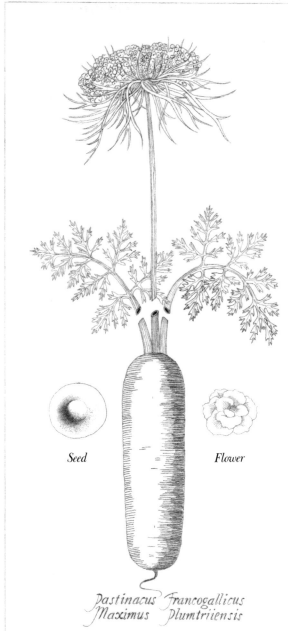

Seed

Flower

Pastinacus Francogallicus
Maximus Plumtriiensis

The PASTINACUS FRANCOGALLICUS MAXI-MUS PLUMTRIIENSIS or PLUMTREES' GIANT FRENCH CARROT is a variety of French CAROTTE developed by P. & W. Plumtree of Tilbury, New Wiltshire, from seed supplied by friends in Dorset, who in turn believed they obtained it from a M. Dupont, unpaid French vice-consul in Asia Minor.

The stem is hollow, corrugated, yellowish-green; flowers clustered, strongly scented, varying in color from white to pale honey; leaves large, smooth, deeply serrated; seeds circular, flat except for slight swelling at center; root strong, straight, untapering, tangerine orange to deep vermillion occasionally flecked with gold.

A most satisfying biannual of exceptional growth and unpredictable habits.

To Eleanor Briggs

From the catalog of P. & W. Plumtree Inc., Seedspeople • Tillbury • New Wiltshire • 037921 • U.S.A.
Reprinted with the kind permission of the proprietors.

Carrot Holes
and
Frisbee Trees

N. M. BODECKER

illustrated by
Nina Winters

A Margaret K. McElderry Book

ATHENEUM   1983   NEW YORK

LIBRARY OF CONGRESS CATALOGING IN PUBLICATION DATA

Bodecker, N. M.
   Carrot holes and frisbee trees.
   "A Margaret K. McElderry book"
   Summary: A gardener and his wife, who want only to
grow an ordinary garden and lead simple lives,
find their carrots growing larger each year,
complicating their lives enormously.
   [1. Carrots—Fiction]   I. Winters, Nina, ill.
II. Title.
PZ7.B63514Car   1983   [Fic]   83-2799
ISBN 0-689-50097-1

Published simultaneously in Canada by McClelland & Stewart, Ltd.
Composition by Dix Type Inc., Syracuse, New York
Printed and Bound by Halliday Lithograph Company, Inc.
West Hanover, Massachusetts
First Edition

Between Newfield and Old Sedum, in the green hills of Tillbury Upper Village, lived a gardener whose name was William
Plumtree and his wife Pippin.

They were much admired, and perhaps a little envied, by the
other villagers, because they grew such very large vegetables.

Everything they planted grew rich and full: cabbages and chard and spinach. But from the very beginning their carrots had grown longer and straighter than any ever seen in Tillbury. And each year they grew larger: the size of soft drink bottles; as big as bowling pins; as large, they said, one year as young penguins. And people took to dropping by in the evening to hear the carrots grow.

So far the Plumtrees were happy, though a little apprehen-

sive. But the year their carrots reached the size of Cub Scouts before the end of June, they began to worry. For how do you pull out a carrot the size of a third-grader? And what do you do with it? And not with just *one* super carrot, but with twenty rows of them; one hundred and twenty carrots to the row; two-thousand-two-hundred-and-forty boy-sized carrots; each weighing eighty-seven pounds. Enough to fill a large, suburban elementary school,

7

two carrots to a desk, with plenty left over for a principal and teachers and dozens of janitors with carrot tops on their heads.

There wasn't room for much else in the Plumtrees' garden. Not even for worms. Well, what *do* you do with such a colossal congregation of carrots? And don't just say: "Eat them!" Imagine eating onehundredandninetyseventhousandninehundredandsixty-seven pounds of boiled carrots! It would take twenty thousand girls and boys more than a year to do that. Just ask your math teacher.

And then there were the holes. A whole garden of holes: four feet deep, and nearly a foot and a half in diameter. The mailman fell into one, the milkman fell into another, and cats and dogs and rubber balls dropped into the rest. The Plumtrees had to post notices:

!DANGER!

CARROT HOLES

and ask people to keep pets and children indoors during the "Hole Season." They had quite a summer, pulling up carrots with block and tackle on a tripod, trimming the tops off with a chain saw, and hauling the trunks to the barn on a wheelbarrow. It was more logging operation than gardening, and the night the last carrot was in, and the last hole filled, they closed the barn doors without a word and went to bed, knowing that some things are better faced in the morning. For what would they do with their barnful of super carrots?

Some they sold to the farmers' market in Dewsbury. The canning factory in New Petersham took twenty truckloads, and tourists bought some as souvenirs. But even after they had sold and given away as many as they could, the woodshed was stuffed to the rafters with carrot logs.

Far into the winter the Plumtrees stood in the shed cutting carrots into sections like cordwood, splitting them with an ax like kindling, carrying it in, dicing it on the chopping board, and cooking and canning every last bit.

As they worked carrot dust and carrot juice got into everything; stuck to their shoes; clung to their clothes; went wherever they went. Their whole world turned orange: orange steam poured out the kitchen windows, filling the air with a perpetual glow of sunrise, and even the snow turned the bright, cheerful color of orange sherbert. Pippin was tempted to sprinkle it with maraschino cherries, to cheer them up. For their whole house, cellar,

attic, and spare bedroom was crammed with canned carrots. Well, carrots arc good for you, they are full of vitamin A.

In the woodshed nothing remained but the pile of half-frozen carrot dust by the sawhorse. Like sawdust, only it tasted a lot better —children on their way to school ate it by the handful.

But by the fire sat Pippin and Plumtree trying not to think of carrots. It wasn't easy, for they had had carrot pancakes with carrot jam and carrot juice for breakfast. They had had carrot soup and a carrot sandwich for lunch; now they were having carrot cake with their carrot tea and something told them that, after a nice carrot supper, they would have some *very* nice carrot sherbert for dessert.

They had tried their carrots every way they could possibly imagine:

> cold, hot, lukewarm, iced,
> sweet, sour, salty, spiced . . .

But carrots will be carrots, and by midwinter they sometimes woke up in the middle of the night having had the most unsettling dreams of grilled cheeseburgers with all sorts of junk on them. And that's pretty far gone for a couple of gardeners.

But there they were, and there the carrots were, and being sensible people, they knew that eating your way through this year's mistake is one way of learning to do better next year. So they ate their nice carrots, and made plans for next summer's garden, while the snow blew around their cottage, the way gardeners have always done. For gardeners are by nature the most optimistic of people.

All right: next year they would pull the carrots up before they got too big and have several crops in a season. Or they would plant just *one* seed, let the thing grow as it would, and have enough carrot for a year. Or they would grow nothing but giant carrots and sell the whole harvest to canning factories. Or they would build a canning factory of their own and get rich. But they didn't *want* a canning factory—and anyway they would have to be rich before they could build one.

It never occurred to them to grow parsley instead. People who garden are funny that way; if they can grow giant cabbages, giant cabbages they grow—even though they hate cabbages.

So they sat reading before the fire while the winter afternoons turned into night and the snow blowing through the hills and woods became invisible in the dark.

One night Plumtree said: "I keep thinking of all those carrot holes. Such a bother to fill and such a waste . . . wish I could think of some use for them."

"I'm sure you will, old Peartree," said Pippin affectionately, without looking up from her book. "You usually do."

But winter went by without Plumtree thinking of anything. The snow melted, the brooks ran full . . .

daffodils like trumpeteers
blew sweet nonsense in their ears . . .

and spring came as the nicest of surprises. The way it always does.

So one morning in April, when it was almost time to plant, Plumtree went out in the field, poking at the soil with the toe of his boot and crumbling handfuls of damp earth—the way gardeners do—and got talking to a neighbor.

The neighbor started in about how he was "gonna put up a fence to keep them varmints out'en his corn," all about the postholes he had to dig, and his aching back, and his blistered hands . . . on and on and on . . . And Plumtree just stood there, squinting at the spring sun, smiling a little, until the other had talked himself out.

"Tell you what," said Plumtree. "I'll grow them for you." The neighbor got cross and said, "You ought to be listenin' better, young fella! I said 'postholes' not 'potatas.'"

"I know," said Plumtree. "And I'll grow them."

The neighbor just glared. So Plumtree explained how it would be done: the seeds would be planted where the posts were going to be; each carrot would be measured as it grew, and when it was the exact dimension of the post, the carrot would come out, and the post would go in. "Nothing to it," said William Plumtree.

"No sweat, no toil, no blisters. As a matter of fact, you could pull up an easy chair and watch your postholes grow."

"Is that a fac'?" said the sour neighbor. "Well, here's another 'fac' for you, MISTER Plumtree: It ain't niver gonna work!"

But a few days later, when he had dug his first three postholes, and thought of the many he still had to dig, he thought that, perhaps, Mister Plumtree's idea *might* work after all.

So the Plumtrees planted the seeds and watered them. And when the first green shoots appeared, the neighbor pulled up his best easy chair and watched his holes grow.

Every morning the carrots were measured; and the moment one reached the right size out it came, and in went the post . . . fitting as tightly as if set in cement. "Well I niver . . ." said the neighbor. And the Plumtrees were in business.

"It's amazing how many holes the world still needs," said Pippin one morning at breakfast. "When you think of the millions and billions already dug and drilled and blasted in it. Fence post-holes, billboard postholes, tobacco field net postholes . . . I made a song about it:

> All the world is full of holes,
> holes for posts and holes for poles:
> May poles, March poles, poles for goals.
> Posts for lamps and laundry-drying,
> poles for Good-Old-Glory-flying.
> (Help, the holes are multiplying!)
> Poles for wires, cables, vines,
> trumpet flowers, power lines,
> mailbox perches, gates, and signs.
> Posts for fencing, swinging, hitching,
> greased-pole-climbing, horseshoe pitching,
> posts that horses use when itching.
> Pole bean pole holes . . .
>   never mind,

I can't go on, but you know what I mean."

And Plumtree did. They were both a little giddy from success, for news had traveled fast that "the Plumtrees have invented a new and easy way of growing holes."

The playschool in Limestock wanted swings and seesaws. "Would the Plumtrees grow the holes?"

"Yes," said Plumtree.

The farmers' market in Barnstead wanted posts for awnings over their stalls . . .

"Yes," said Plumtree.

Ginghamton wanted holes for road signs . . . Dwarfing wanted utility poles . . . Woolsum wanted gate posts, and Candlebury wanted a new flagstaff.

"Yes," "Perhaps," and "Maybe . . ." said Plumtree.

"No!" said Pippin. "It's too much."

For ever since they'd started growing holes, they had been on the go from dawn till after dark. PLUMTREE'S POSTHOLES INC. was big business and hard, exacting work. If a carrot was pulled out too late, the post wobbled; if it was pulled too soon the post wouldn't go in. They raced all over Macintosh County with their tripod, seeds, yardsticks, and watering cans and had no time for their own garden. Watering it before dawn and pulling weeds at midnight was not the best way to do it.

They had thought of hiring someone to go around and measure carrots while they worked their garden. A carrot-hole-growth-checker. But soon they might need more, and more . . . and before anyone could say, "Pippin Plumtree," they would be involved in an enormous business, growing holes all over the state, perhaps all over the country: Des Moines, Memphis, Buffalo, N.Y. . . .

When all they *really* wanted was to grow vegetables, bring them to market, and take things as they came.

Instead they were wearing themselves out, growing holes "the easy way." They sat down on the porch steps and made two decisions: 1. They would accept no more orders for holes that year; and 2. only half as many next year.

They seemed like good decisions. But when Pippin began thinking of all the backaches suffered by people digging holes, she was not so sure. "We have the perfect hole-grower, and I don't think we can keep it to ourselves just because we don't want a big business. It isn't right."

"True," said Plumtree. "But we can't grow all the holes the world needs by ourselves either." So there they were.

It was Pippin who thought of the way out, or at least the beginning of it.

One morning when they were pulling out a carrot at the post office in South Mulchboro, she suddenly stopped pulling on the chain and said: "What about mail-order holes?" "What?" said Plumtree. "Well, we simply mail people the seeds— PLUMTREE'S PATENTED POSTHOLE GROWER KIT, or something—with instructions on how to use them. All *we* do is grow them and mail them."

"Hm," said Plumtree, and "Maybe . . ."

Each year they left two super carrots in the ground through the winter, one on either side of the front door. The tops stayed

green long after frost, and in early spring the roots sent up new shoots that grew rapidly and in a few weeks overshadowed the house. In June the carrot trees bloomed—thousands of white, honey-scented flowers like giant Queen Anne's lace. By late August the seeds for next year's crop were ready for harvest. They were round and flat and the size of saucers.

When the wind blew through the carrot tops, seeds sailed over the house like Frisbees. And when the wind didn't blow, the children asked Pippin to "shake the Frisbee tree."

Driving out of Mulchboro that early summer morning Plumtree said, "If we left two whole rows in this winter, we should have enough seeds for your mail-order plan. But wouldn't we be spending all our time wrapping and mailing? And wouldn't we need a regular carrot-seed wrappery? and carrot-seed wrappers? and mailing room clerks and typists and secretaries? Maybe even conveyer belts and seed-sorting machines? We would live in a factory."

"We would need a bigger barn too," said Pippin. "And harvesters, and vans to take parcels to the post office. Old Woolcloth couldn't handle it alone (Woolcloth was the postmaster), *he* would need help too—and a bigger post office, new and bare and ugly."

She sat very quietly looking out the window as they drove down the green valley along the river, through Colebrook and Barnsfield, and up the steep, rutted dirt road to the hill country: Gillmantown and Aster and Crowsfoot Notch. From there she caught a glimpse of their own quiet village nestled in the trees and

24

thought, a little sadly, how its peace would be gone forever if they built their factory.

They thought and they thought, but whatever they thought of sooner or later would become Big Business.

So the summer went by, fall came, and they began their harvest, walking about in the sun with a large basket between them, collecting the seeds.

In the afternoon they played Frisbee with one of the seeds, and Pippin said: "We could also make a carrot-seed-Frisbee-factory . . ." "No," said Plumtree. ". . . and make that a mail-order business, too," said Pippin. "PLUMTREE'S FRISBEE TREE STARTER KIT, just add water and watch." "No!" said Plumtree. "Stop it!"

But Pippin would not be stopped. "Have you ever thought what would happen if these things grew wild? A world full of giant carrot trees and wild Frisbees? I think of it almost every night." Then she sat down on the steps and said, "Sorry, 'Tree, I just wish we could give the whole thing away."

"But who would we give it to?" said Plumtree.

So they went back to work. But when they emptied the last basket into the bin, Plumtree said, "Suppose we mailed all the gardeners we know one box of seeds each, asking *them* to mail *their* spare seeds to all the gardeners *they* know—in a few years

26

super carrots would be everywhere. No more digging, no more backaches, but food and shade trees and Frisbees too."

So that's what they did: they mailed ninety-seven boxes to thirty-four states, plus one to Kenya, and one to the Isle of Man.

And then Plumtree got sick.

He was in the hospital a long while, and Pippin did their work alone.

One day on a visit she said, "There is a very large carrot growing in the lawn, it must have seeded itself. I'm not sure what to do . . ."

"It was for a dovecote posthole, a surprise for your birthday; but I forgot," said Plumtree.

"Well, surprise!" said Pippin. "I got a shade tree instead."

But the carrot in the lawn was very *very* big. And while Plumtree was away it *grew* and GREW . . . it was by far the largest carrot ever.

When Plumtree came home, in the first deep freeze of winter, the huge carrot-top tree was turning yellow—but the carrot continued to grow. At night they heard the ground creaking and in the morning found deep cracks in the frozen lawn. The turf was rising, like frost heaves, from the pressure of the giant growing below.

It was too late to pull it out now the ground was frozen. Anyway, their tripod would have been much too small. They needed a full-size crane like the ones builders use. They lay awake at night listening to the "carrot heaves," wondering what would happen next, but when snow came, the rumbling ceased. Perhaps the carrot had finally stopped growing; perhaps it was only the snow muffling the sound. Who could tell?

Once more they sat by the fire laying out the summer's work. They had long lists of people who wanted holes, all over Macintosh and Baldwin counties, in Hillsum and Woolsum and Lambsted and Cornbridge Junction. Even as far away as Lymeburne and North Sleeting on the far side of The Ridge.

Things were getting quite complicated. They stuck flags in maps and wrote notes in calendars:

4th June

    7:30 A.M. East Primsett. Mr. Parnip. 12 holes for a kennel.

    8:45 Linsington. Miss Emerson. Mailbox post.

    9:15 Tuncaster. Flagstaff. (on green)

    9:55 Mulchboro/Mulchboro Center. Six utility poles.

    10:30 Gingham. Two posts for honor roll.

    11:25 Gingham State Park. 57 fence posts. Road to Ginghamton . . .

And so on, and so on, all summer long. But seen from the safe distance of a winter afternoon fire, it didn't look too bad, and if it hadn't been for that giant carrot in the lawn, all would have been peaceful. But they kept having nightmares about it and even

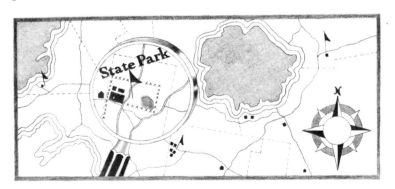

got up in the middle of the night and went out in the deep snow with a flashlight to see what it was up to.

The shadows of the huge carrot fronds swept silently over the snow, like the tail of a cat watching a goldfish . . . but all was quiet. So they crept back to bed, cold and not reassured. They knew that *ordinary* carrots live only two seasons: during the first the root stores all the strength needed to produce flowers and seeds the second—then it dies. But this was no ordinary carrot. It might go on growing forever . . . splitting the ground open like a slow earthquake . . . swallowing their house.

Pippin began thinking of it as MONSTER CARROT, something awful they had started and couldn't control. It was going to take over! First *their* garden; then their neighbor's; then all of Tillbury Upper Village and Tillbury Lower Village. The seeds would Frisbee everywhere: there would be MONSTER CARROTS in the fields, MONSTER CARROTS in the hills, MONSTER CARROTS in the school yards and playgrounds. The seeds would fly farther and farther from county to county, till the entire state was a dense, dismal forest of MONSTER CARROTS, crisscrossed by dark crevices inhabited only by ENORMOUS MOTHS and FABULOUS CATERPILLARS.

"Stop it, Pippin!" said Plumtree. But his imagination was working too. What if the monsters did take over? What if they became pests rather than blessings?

When the snow melted new green shoots appeared on the monster, growing very rapidly—a foot and a half a day—but the carrot itself had stopped growing. Or had it?

They worried, but during spring planting were too busy to do anything about it. And when at last they had the time, the only crane in the county big enough to handle the monster was booked till October. They listened anxiously first thing in the morning and again before going to bed. Some days there were rumblings, other days all was quiet.

But the carrot tree in the lawn had grown so large and so beautiful that they almost hoped it would keep growing.

Sunday mornings they breakfasted under it. Noontimes they lay in its shade listening to the bees. Evenings they sat under it, sniffing the odd, heady scent of carrot flowers, which becomes almost overpowering—like honeysuckle—when the dew falls.

And they nearly forgot the monster below.

When the first seeds landed in the grass, though, they took no chances, but made quite sure *every single one* of them went into the special bin in the barn. The seeds were as large as dinner plates, and when they skimmed over the chimney at dusk, it was easy to believe in flying saucers. But the crickets sang in the fields at night, and all was peace.

Until one evening, just before they went in, there was a deep, booming rumble in the earth, and the lawn trembled . . .

They jumped into their pickup and drove straight to the crane people in New Petersham—and the crane people said, "We'll be right over."

But a crane does not travel very fast, even on a flatbed truck, and it was nearly two o'clock in the morning before it came up Old Sedum Road, with the Petersham police cruiser in front, lights flashing, and the fire trucks from Mulchboro and Prim and Dwarfing snailing close behind. Followed by an empty flatbed for the monster.

Everything looked unreal in the flashing lights and jumping shadows: the crane's long skeleton neck and small dinosaur head swaying over the treetops, in search of its prey; the black carrot fronds swishing the night air as if a hurricane were brewing; the fire engines, half-hidden in the lane, rumbling dangerously like square-necked bulls straining to use their strength.

The villagers appeared silently, not knowing what to expect. For the moment the monster was quiet. It seemed that whatever was going on underground came and went like a deep-rooted toothache.

Pippin and Plumtree stood a little away from the rest, waiting. The whole operation was like pulling a very large, very bad tooth. What if the tooth was stronger than the crane? What if the chain broke? What if the crane broke? "Never mind, Pippin," said Plumtree; but he moved back a little farther into the shadows.

The head crane man clambered all over the base of the carrot

tree with his helpers, fastening his hooks and linking his chains. The firemen aimed their hoses; the policemen stood ready to blow their whistles—though no one knew quite why.

"A big 'un all right," said the crane man full of awe. "But out she'll come! Yes *sir!* This here crane of mine will have 'er out in no time flat. No two ways about it!" But when the struggle began, it appeared that there might be two ways about it after all: the crane's AND the carrot's. The crane roared and strained, but the carrot gave not an inch.

The crane moved closer, pulling longer and harder—but the carrot held its ground.

The crane lumbered around, like a huge, frantic bird tugging at a worm, while the crane man clanked his gears and levers, and the caterpillar tracks churned up the ground.

But the carrot held on.

For a few moments all was quiet. No one spoke, and nothing moved except the flashing lights in the lane. The crane man stood up, wiped his face, stretched, and flexed his muscles as if *he, personally,* were going to pull out the monster.

Then he had one last go. The crane's neck arched back, shivering like a fly rod landing a trout. It looked as if all the rivets and bars and girders would snap . . .

"No!" cried Pippin from somewhere in the eerie shadows.

But instead there was a deep, heaving sigh, as the monster finally gave up the struggle.

And there it came: rising out of the ground, *the shape and size of a factory chimney!*

Thirty-two feet long, four feet across. Looking almost like pure gold in the full glow of the sunrise.

"Golly!" said the crane man.

By the time the crane and the carrot had left—each on its flatbed truck, led by the police cruiser and followed by the fire trucks, all with their lights flashing yellow and blue and red—it was broad daylight. And the villagers, who had stood gaping after the caravan as it wound its way downhill through Sedum and Waybrook to Petersham Mill, had gone home.

Only Woolcloth, the postmaster, joined the Plumtrees at the edge of the hole. He dropped a pebble into it, and after a few moments they heard the unmistakable "plop" of a small object hitting water. "Well," said Woolcloth, "this time it appears that you have grown a well! Line it with cement rings, and you are in

business. Lovely mornin' Pippin. Pip-pip, 'Tree." And he too went home to bed.

But Pippin and Plumtree went down through the fields to a pond called Gorse Pond, where they sometimes swam in the morning. It was too cold now—yellow and red leaves covered the water —but they sat in the grass all morning, watching the dragonflies and the bluets, and keeping as quiet as they could.

Postholes. Shade trees. Frisbees. And now wells! Where would it all end?

Later in the day, as they walked back uphill toward the house, they heard the telephone ringing a great distance off. Ringing on and on in the empty house, as if it were trying to call them back. They were still thinking of the monster they had sent to the sawmill to be cut up and perhaps used for firewood. For there is the strange thing about carrots, that if they are left in the ground a second year and allowed to bloom, they turn hard and woody before they finally rot away. So why not use them in the stove?

When they got back to the house the phone was still ringing steadily, and when they picked it up the sawmill man was shouting

at the other end, "Pippin? 'Tree? That you? Where you been all mornin'? You listenin', hey? Wow! Have I got news for you! You revolutionized the lumber industry! That's what you done. Jus' cuttin' up that monster of yourn. Carrot wood, fellas! Hard as oak, straight as pine. Boards three feet wide and never a knot hole nowhere! You've grown lumber in two years that an oak couldn't grow in two hundred. Think of it, fellas! Think . . ."

And think they did. The more they tried to give this thing away, the more it grew on them, as if the carrot was trying to tell them something: That you can't give your luck away? Or that you shouldn't try?

All they really wanted was to grow a garden and live plain, simple lives.

"But maybe if you are given something, you are supposed to do something with it," said Pippin. "Like people who can paint pictures or discover cures for things. If you are especially good at something, that's what you have to do."

And that's what they did. They grew postholes and shade trees and Frisbees and wells and cordwood and timber—and lived busily ever after.

What happened to their parsley another year . . . now that is *quite* a different story.

JJ   85-9204

Bodecker
Carrot Holes and Frisbee Trees

Date Due
